BLOOD
AND
GUTS

TR ISHAM

ISBN: 0692496149
ISBN-13: 978-0692496145

Entrails Press

-1-
BURNT FLESH

"Another stupid trip to the stupid, stank zoo," Russ muttered as he searched his backpack for the permission slip.

"What's that, Russell?" asked Ms. Platt. She could give her voice an angry edge that sliced through all of the chatter in a classroom. Suddenly all of the other kids were looking at him.

"What!" He zipped up his backpack while the rest of them stood there with their slips in hand, watching him.

"You know, Russell," Platt said in her softer, crouching-panther voice, "you could always stay here and catch up on all that homework you owe me."

"Wh-" he started again, but Platt cut in.

"MATH! JOURNALS OUT!" she barked in a voice loud enough to make them all jump. "Zoo bus leaves in 40 minutes, and we *will* finish these fractions!"

The rest of them rapidly stuffed their permission slips in the basket on Platt's desk and scurried back to their seats. Somehow, Russ was the the last one ready for math, and Platt let him know about it with a long, dead stare, followed by an "I give up" sigh.

Another awesome day of school.

On the way to the zoo, as an extra little *gotcha*, Platt made him sit in the front seat, the one right across from her. It was a 40-minute ride, window jammed, legs sticking to the green vinyl seat. Video games were banned from the bus, but he still had his iPod, blasting Megadeth into his skull. He knew that heavy metal really bothered Platt and that she could probably hear it. He turned it up and smirked.

When they got there and stepped out onto the griddle of the zoo's parking lot, Platt stopped right in front of him, eyes bulging in a *what-do-you-think-you're-doing* stare. He realized he was still wearing his headphones, still blaring. He hit pause and asked, "Can't I just keep it?"

Ms. Platt took a deep breath through her nostrils, closed her eyes, then turned on her heel and walked on. It was one of those times where she was just too sick of him to argue.

He switched to Portishead for the tour, because it was blazing hot and Megadeth was only making the heat worse. The music helped block out Platt and the tour guide, but it couldn't block out his least favorite part of the zoo: the smell.

The air was thick and sticky with the essence of a hundred animals relieving themselves on damp cement in hundred-degree heat. He could almost *see* the urine in the syrupy heat wiggling up from the pavement. To top it off, each and every animal was sleeping. If only that had stopped them from defecating. But, as his nose told him, it hadn't.

He was wishing for the 100th time that he had brought nose plugs, when he noticed something. The smell of a zoo, like a thousand public toilets in each sniff, was everywhere. But this was different.

He smelled burning.

He looked around to see if he could find smoke, yearning for the excitement that a burning building would bring. Though that would have made the zoo trip totally worthwhile, he knew that wasn't it. He recognized the smell, and it wasn't wood burning, it was meat. And there was another aspect to the odor, one he recognized only because he had accidentally burned his eyebrows off last summer playing with lighter fluid: burning hair.

He quickly scanned the nearby cages for burning animals. He almost missed it, but there, behind the concrete edge of the tiger cage, he saw black crust on a brown-furred animal, something about the size of a small dog. As he stared, he could just make out a few pinpricks of twinkling orange embers.

He didn't have much time to think about it as his earbuds were yanked from his head. He spun around to see Ms. Platt clenching a white-knuckled fist around the cord and extending the other hand in an upturned palm. The look on her face was beyond rage, and, as much as he enjoyed messing with deserving teachers, her look told him that this was not the time. He placed his iPod in her open hand and ran to catch up with the rest of the class way over at the outdoor section of the monkey building.

Once there, he looked back to see Platt stalking furiously toward him. Over her shoulder, he could just barely see the burnt thing.

The wavy haze of hot pavement made it tough to be sure, but he was almost positive: it moved.

It didn't seem alive, but it slid slowly out of sight, like it was being dragged.

-2-

DUMB QUESTIONS

Deprived of his iPod, Russ couldn't help but hear the same boring speeches he had heard a dozen times before. Did you know bald eagles use the same nest every year and just add more twigs and junk to it? Did you know that zebras are actually *black* with *white* stripes? Hey, guess what, bats *always* turn left when they leave their caves! You'll be shocked and amazed to hear that wolves have many different howls they use to communicate with their pack! And did you ever hear how the ringtailed Polynesian donglefish eats thumbtacks and motor oil and then farts the national anthem of Finland?

It was tough for Russ to resist rolling his eyes as the tour guide soldiered on, dressed in khaki and olive drab, pockets bulging with God-knows-what. The strap on her pith helmet was strung taut, her posture rigid, like a soldier at attention.

The only part of her getup that seemed less than military-grade was the red box of animal crackers hanging around her neck on a shoelace. Russ studied it as she blathered on and discovered tiny holes punched in it, probably a dark, jostling prison for some small, unlucky critter.

How could she be so militantly enthusiastic about saying the same old wacky animal facts for the millionth time? How could she believe anyone would still want to hear them?

But some people did, and most of those people were the F.O.D.'s. Darla Collins was in Ms. Platt's class with Russ, and she thought she was hot snot. The *hottest* of snot. So did a group of four or five girls who hung on her every word, bought clothes from the same stores she did, and tried to style their hair like hers. Russ didn't even know these girls' names, so in his head he just called them F.O.D.'s, Friends of Darla.

Darla was in the front row, wide-eyed and fascinated by every word out of the tour guide's mouth, and so were four nearly-identical F.O.D.'s. Even the tour guide seemed a little creeped out by it.

The tour guide, in her mercy, was actually wrapping it up. Then she said the thing Russ was hoping she wouldn't: "So, does anyone have any questions?"

She wasn't even done pronouncing the word "questions" before Darla Collins' hand shot up earnestly, followed by the hands of the F.O.D.'s. Then, the mind-numbing Q and A.

Q: Do you have a favorite animal?
A: I like them all, but I think the tortoises are my favorite!

(Russ figured she picked the dullest animal in the zoo to try to get kids interested in it.)

Q: What made you want to be a zookeeper?
A: (Chuckle) I'm not exactly a zookeeper, but I guess I just always liked animals. I think they're fascinating blah blah blah...

Q: Do you name the animals?
A: Not officially, no, but some of us call them names anyway!
(Russ had some names for them: Sleepy, Boring, Toilet-stench...)

Q: How come we couldn't see the cute little otters today, not even sleeping?
A: The otters weren't in their cage today, they're most likely getting cared for in our "animal hotel." They might need shots!
Follow-up Question: Squeeeeeeal!

Q: What do the animals eat?

A: They actually eat all different sorts of things! Here in our "zoo kitchen," we prepare blah blah blah...

This was always the longest and most boring answer of the tour, but someone always asked the question. Food, thought Russ. They eat food.

Then his mind snapped back to the burnt whatever-it-was behind the tiger cage, and he had a question of his own.

"Do any of the animals like their food cooked? Or burned?"

The F.O.D.'s giggled, and even the tour guide cracked a smile. "Heh, no! Animals in nature don't know how to use stoves, so, heh! So no, we don't cook for them here!" Ms. Platt was enjoying the laugh at Russ's expense.

He was furious, and wanted answers. "Well, then how did... I mean, I *saw*..." He trailed off though, remembering that the corpse had been dragged away, so he might have no proof. The whole class and the tour guide were openly laughing at Russ now. He wanted to crawl into a hole.

As the class shuffled off toward the parking lot, he grabbed Ms. Platt's sleeve and asked for his iPod back.

"Here," she said, shoving it at him, "I'm tired of carrying this. *Now*," she said, crouching to get her face close to his, her voice low and threatening, "I don't want to see or hear you for the rest of this trip." Palatable fumes of stale coffee overwhelmed him, and Platt's bloodshot eyes stared directly into his. "I don't even want to know you're here."

She slowly rose to her full height, taller than most men he knew, and blocked the afternoon sun. She turned and walked away. Russ looked back toward the lion cage, but it was too far to see. Would there be scorch marks on the pavement? Burnt guts?

He wanted to go check it out, but he did not want to be in more trouble. He hated the idea of getting back on that bus, and the thought of getting back to school in time for social studies made him nauseous. He also hated the thought of everyone laughing at him, thinking he was stupid for asking his dumb question and the way he stammered with his follow-up question.

Russ looked up and saw Platt swaggering away, like the victor in a colosseum battle.

Russ ran.

-3-
LEFT BEHIND

The first voice Russ expected to hear was Platt yelling after him, but instead it was a fat man whose slurpy he spilled accidentally.

"Hey watch it kid!"

His wife, looking at the crimson stains which had splashed onto her white shorts, shouted "No *running*! At the *zoo*!"

In her moment of rage, she looked like a lot like a screeching monkey, and Russ giggled as he darted down a path between two buildings. He stopped to catch his breath, hands on his knees, sweat pouring down his temples. What was he doing?

He was in a shaded alley between the elephant building and the one with the cockroaches that also looked out onto the otter enclosure. There were restrooms and a drinking fountain.

While he was greedily slurping the lukewarm trickle from the spigot, he realized someone was talking to him.

"What are you doing here? Aren't you taking the bus?"

He turned to find an F.O.D. drying her hands on her plaid pink shorts, the same shade of pink as her visor and her little rolled-up socks.

"Aren't you?" he spat back. His legs tensed as he prepared to take off again.

"My mom came to pick me up," she said, tucking her visor into her armpit so she could scoop her hair into a ponytail, "and she said we could stay longer. Are you getting picked up, too?"

"No, uh…" Russ was not a quick thinker. "I mean, uh…" He realized it was too late to lie. "Leave me alone!"

"What? They're all going to be looking for you! You are going to be in *huge* trouble!" She seemed genuinely distressed.

"So what!" he shouted and stalked off. He hated her and her stupid socks, her stupid ponytail, and her stupid mom.

Walking out of the shade was like walking into an oven, so he took a quick right into the otter building. He walked over to the cockroach terrarium and watched them slowly crawl over the branches like little machines, segmented legs and shells gleaming in the fluorescent light. They were incredible to him with their tiny, meticulous bodies and utterly unknowable minds.

"Of course *you're* looking at the bugs, Russell," huffed the F.O.D., who had followed him in. She knew his name, which made it awkward for him that he didn't know hers. He knew what she meant: weird kids like weird animals, and nice kids like otters.

"Why aren't you going all doe-eyed at the window?" he asked. The window was partially submerged in the pond, so you could see the otters being cute on land or underwater.

"Otters are *smart*," she snapped, cheeks flushing, "they use rocks like *tools* to crack open clams! I'd like to see a roach do that!"

Russ winced. The zoo had a river otter. She must have seen sea otters on TV once and thought all otters were the same.

"What!" she demanded, folding her arms, "Are you going to tell me that roaches use tools too? Cause they don't!" She whipped her pink-ribboned ponytail around and began walking away, then turned to deliver another message: "And for your information, the otter isn't in his cage today! He's probably at the animal ho-TEL!"

He couldn't see how this message applied to him, but he was seething nonetheless. He looked back at the Madagascar hissing cockroaches, their measured, mechanical movements, and started to calm down. That's when it came to him; he knew. And he had the perfect comeback to the F.O.D., and to all otterkind: "It's not in the animal hospital. It's dead."

-4-
BUSTED

Her look of surprise, wide eyes and open mouth, cheeks flushed pink, was the greatest thing Russ had seen at the zoo all day.

Finally, she found her voice: "Russell Yamhill, you shut up! That is not true!"

He was enjoying this, so he took his time before replying, with a little smile, "Sure it is. I can even prove it!"

She was irate now, pausing between each word, "No... you... can't!"

"Come with me," he said, "if you don't believe me." He walked out without looking back.

Cheered by his triumph, he hummed and walked briskly over to the tiger cage. He was definitely in huge trouble for ditching the class, but that was already done. While he was waiting for the hammer to fall, he could at least satisfy his curiosity.

A maintenance man in coveralls and a hat, pushing a cart loaded with cleaning supplies, gave Russ the hairy eyeball as he rounded the back corner of the Tiger cage. Russ had to pretend to be very interested in the trees until the maintenance man left.

Eventually he did, scowling beneath his bushy moustache, and Russ turned his attention to the pavement. It reminded him of art class, when they had drawn with charcoal, dragging chalky hunks of it across the paper to make those heavy, impossibly black marks. That's what he was looking at now, a charcoal smear.

Except this one had guts.

Streaked in the black were pink and gray, glistening morsels of liver and kidneys, and tubes of intestine twisting up like stems of weird pink plants. There was fur here and there, sprouting at odd angles, and a paw. A tiny forepaw, frozen in death as it grasped at the air.

"Gross!" The F.O.D. startled him, he hadn't noticed her coming up behind him. "What *is* that?" Her face crumpled like a tissue and she covered her mouth.

Russ stood tall, chin held high, and deeply inhaled the scent of burnt fur. "That," he said, extending his hand toward the black streak and looking her dead in the eye, "is your North American river otter."

"No it's not!" she screeched, turning her head. "You're so *mean*! Why are you so mean!"

Crouching, he pointed to a tuft of brown fur sticking out of the black stripe.

"It's a raccoon!" she said, "Just a stupid squirrel or something!"

Then, his coup de grace. Using his thumb and forefinger ever so delicately, Russ reached down and plucked the paw from the mess. Holding it by one finger, he displayed it before her: it was a tiny, webbed paw with five little claws. Unmistakably otterish. There were a few charred threads of vein dangling from the wrist.

He thought she would scream, hoped she would scream, but she only cried. Her shoulders lurched as she sobbed behind her hands.

"Geez, sorry," said Russ. Her crying took all the fun out of his win. "It's just a..." he stopped himself before he said *stupid*. "Just an otter."

She wiped her eyes and stood up straight. "We have to tell the zoo people. Come on, let's find my mom."

He was about to tell her to go play in traffic, that he wasn't looking for anyone's mom about now, but he felt guilty for making her cry. So he just nodded.

Before they could even start, though, there came a voice that split their eardrums like a hatchet: "WHERE HAVE YOU BEEN!?"

Standing over them, hand on her hips, lips peeled back from her teeth and red eyes glaring, stood Ms. Platt.

Her gaze fell to the mess on the pavement, then back to Russ. She seemed to actually vibrate with rage. Her eyes looked positively insane.

"WHAT DID YOU DO!?"

-5-

TACKLED & SHACKLED

Russ felt his stomach shrivel like a raisin, and he doubled over. The F.O.D. was one of those good kids that was so good, she became upset even if someone standing near her got in trouble. She squirmed and looked guilty.

"RUSSEL! I..." Platt stopped mid-scream and looked up. A couple of khaki-clad zoo workers and two police officers walked quickly toward them, shooing them toward the exit along with a couple dozen other confused and irritated people.

"Ma'am, ma'am please, this way..." one of the officers said to Ms. Platt in a voice similar to the one Platt used on the class when they were acting up.

Russell looked up and saw similar interactions all over, confounded people getting urged toward the exit by police and zoo employees.

Platt was trying to say something, but they ushered her on. Russ and the F.O.D. had no choice but to go along, though in the growing current of people they separated from Platt. They saw her above the crowd, jumping up to keep track of Russ and trying to call out. The cops near her (now there were three) raised their hands and repeated, "Ma'am, Ma'am, please. Ma'am..."

But she just couldn't stand being told what to do, and she blew a gasket. "LET... ME... GO!" she roared, squirming away from them, a wild, flailing hand smacking an officer dead in the face, sending his hat flying.

The whole crowd stopped to look as the cops quickly had her facedown on the filthy zoo ground, clicking her big wrists into a shiny set of handcuffs. They jerked her to her feet, an officer at each elbow, and dragged her onward. Just beyond the fence, in the parking lot, was the school bus, which erupted in cheers.

Russ didn't dare cheer, even though it was the single greatest moment of his life so far. He and the F.O.D. just went along with the crowd.

As they were passing the monkey house, he felt a sharp yank on his arm and was pulled in. He was momentarily overwhelmed by a sense of doom, until he saw that it was the F.O.D. who had pulled him.

"Alright," she whispered, "What is going on here?" Each entrance to the monkey house had a large vestibule with displays. This one was rainforest-themed, with terrariums and aquariums along the walls. Her jaw was clenched and her face was red. She was perturbed.

"Uh, I don't... um," he stammered. Russ was not good under pressure. Apparently she thought he had some answers.

"Why are they evacuating the zoo? What happened to the otter? And why are you still holding that hand?" She pointed angrily at his right hand, which was still, to his surprise, holding the otter paw.

Unsure of what to tell her, he handed over the paw. She cradled it in her palms like a baby chick. "Aww..." she cooed. "It'll never crack another clam again!"

He couldn't take it any more. "It never *did* crack a clam! Clams live in the *ocean*! They get opened and eaten by *sea otters*! That was a *river otter*!"

She threw it at him, it bounced off his cheek and plopped into the piranha tank. She was crying again, softly.

"Look, um..." he started, but faltered. "uh, *you*..."

She looked at him and her face slowly bloomed with realization, then frosted over with contempt. "You don't even know my name!" Her ears blazed crimson. "Russell David Yamhill! I've been in the same class as you for two years! And you don't even know my name! And now I'm stuck in here with all of these disgusting snakes and I have no idea where my mom even is!" At the word "mom," her voice cracked. She turned her back to him and folded her arms.

He wanted to ask her name, but, instead, he said, "Sea otters sleep together, floating, for safety." No response. "They hold hands so they won't drift apart."

She turned back around and sniffed. "Really?"

"Yeah," he continued, "they link up their little paws and hang on while they sleep."

She giggled despite her misery. "Well, now what? I guess we just go find a cop and ask about my mom."

"Aren't you curious, though? About what the big deal is?" He could see she was. "Come on!" He ran into the monkey house, through the long central hall, and crouched by the back door, the one facing the otter building. This vestibule was desert-themed, and a gila monster flicked its black tongue behind the glass near his head.

She ran and crouched across from him. "What now?"

"Well, let's wait here until it clears out, then run back there to see if we can see what's up," he said, pointing toward the back of the zoo.

"Okay," she said. "But then I'm finding my mom!"

"Okay," he said. "Um..."

She gave an exasperated sigh and said, "*Amy.*"

-6-
NICE SHOT

"Stay down!" whispered Russ, but Amy insisted on inching up the wall to peek out the circular window in the door. She took off her pink visor and peered carefully over the bottom rim.

"What can you see? Are they all gone?" Russ whispered. She shooed away his questions with a wave of her hand.

She heard a delicate tap behind her and turned slowly to see a dinner-plate sized tarantula with its forelegs on the glass beside her head.

She screamed and covered her mouth almost immediately. She dropped back to the floor, eyes wide in panic. Russ rolled his eyes. Some kids were so squeamish.

"There's a police officer out there!" she whispered, panic in her features. "He had his back to me, but what if he heard me?"

"Well," he whispered back, "maybe if you hadn't squealed because of a stupid spider..."

"Shut up!" she snapped back. "We gotta run!"

"No," Russ said, "he'd hear our footsteps. Scooch over here, against this door." Russ knew that one side of almost every double-door entrance in the zoo was locked. He just hoped he had picked the right one this time.

They huddled against the door, listening, trying not to even breathe. She smelled like bubblegum and hairspray. They could hear heavy footsteps on the asphalt, coming closer.

"Hello?" came a man's voice from the other side. "Anyone in there?" Then, they could feel the door pressing against their backs. Russ tensed up, ready to run. Amy held her head in her hands.

"What?" yelled the officer. "Yeah," he continued, still talking loudly with someone farther away, probably another cop. "No, yeah, I'll be right there. Thought I heard something in here."

Russ and Amy could hear the other voice, but not clearly. They could make out the words "polar bear," "evacuate," and they heard it say "never seen anything like it!"

"Yeah, totally disgusting, real sick puppy!" yelled the officer on the other side of the door. "This one's locked, I'm gonna walk around to the side door, sweep the building. I'll meet you out front."

His footsteps receded.

Amy's head snapped up and stared Russ right in the eyes. Before he could even think, she grabbed his arm and yanked, and they were out the door, sprinting toward the path leading to the back half of the zoo, toward the polar bears.

She dragged him behind some tall trees beside the wallaby area, and they both stopped to catch their breath, hands on their knees.

After a minute, he asked, still panting, "What was that? Are you crazy?"

"Didn't you," she started, then paused to breathe. "Didn't you hear? He was going to come in! The *side*!"

"Well yeah, but..." he couldn't finish that argument. She had done the only thing they could have done. She had saved him. He had no idea why, but that made him angry.

"We have to see the polar bears, did you hear?" he asked.

"Yes I heard, Russell." she spat back. "But look!" There were two police between the wallaby and the big, fake-rock entrance to the polar bear display. There was also a man in a suit and sunglasses standing right by the door.

"Come on," he said. "The side entrance."

She looked at him quizzically.

"You know, over by the pheasant?" he said. She still didn't show any sign of recognition. "In the hill?"

Russ walked abruptly off in the direction of the pheasants, bent low. He didn't care if she followed or not. He rounded the hill carefully, almost tiptoeing, as the pheasant cage came slowly into view. No cops.

He noticed her behind him as he snuck up on the small door in the side of the hill. It was rusted and gray, and there was no label on it.

"Are you sure this goes to the bears?" she whispered.

Russ just looked at her, thinking *haven't you ever been to the zoo before*? He rolled his eyes and shook his head. The doorknob squeaked slightly as he turned it, and he froze. He listened for footsteps, heard none, and pushed gently.

The welcome chill of air conditioning swept out to welcome them, and they slipped in.

It was dark inside, especially on the far side from the bear tank. It was a larger version of the otter display, with a huge pane of glass showing views both above and below the water. Most of the light in the vast room was filtered through the water, giving the place a blue, wavering glow. It took their eyes a minute to adjust.

They could see the silhouettes of five men in front of the water, three police and two more guys in suits. Russ and Amy huddled behind a trash can in the darkest part of the room, near where they had snuck in.

She looked at him and raised her hands, palms up, in a "What are we gonna do now?" gesture.

Russ had seen countless movies with scenes like this, where the character throws a rock, making a diversionary noise, and then sneaks onto the scene as the guards run off to investigate. He looked around, no rock.

Amy, seeming to have read his mind, pointed at something sticking out of the wall. It was a short, thick metal arm meant to stop the doorknob from slamming into the wall.

Russ reached down and twisted. With maximum effort, he got it started, the continued to carefully unscrew it until it fell into his hand. He was surprised how heavy it was, and he wondered how far he'd be able to throw it. It was about the size of a hot dog, and felt as heavy as a brick.

As two years of little league had taught him, Russ was a terrible shot. He wanted to hit the doors, the main entrance, hoping they would all rush there.

He stood up, drew his right arm slowly back, the door stopper cold and heavy in his hand. Russ took a deep breath, focused his eyes on the doors, and fired.

He watched, helpless as it sailed several yards left of the doors. So far left, in fact, that it hit one of the police officers squarely in the back of the head.

-7-

WHAT HAPPENED TO THE BEAR?

It hit his skull with a dull ring, then thumped quietly on the thick carpet. Amy's eyes were so wide they seemed about to pop out of her skull, and Russ, for the first time in his life, had a strong and sincere desire to be in social studies.

Just then, all of the police radios in the room crackled to life at once: "ALL UNITS ALL UNITS!" There was a lot of loud static, a bunch of numbers were shouted, then: "WE FOUND ONE! REPEAT! WE FOUND ONE! ALIVE!"

Both men in suits and two of the cops were out the front door in less than two Mississippis, too fast to notice the third officer.

He stood and swayed, like a toddler late for a nap, then he just folded up like a lawn chair and lay down, his cop hat rolling a few feet away before coming to rest.

"You killed him!" Amy said, no longer trying to be quiet. "Why did you do that!?"

He was too shocked to explain that he couldn't have hit that man in the head if he'd tried, not if he'd had a million chances, never in a million years. He had failed to even hit the entrance, at which he'd carefully focused his aim, the three sets of double doors at the entrance which were probably 12 feet wide altogether.

While these things were going through his head, Amy was kneeling beside the fallen officer. "He's breathing," she said nervously.

Russ walked over to stand behind her, creeping up to the unconscious man as if he were a sleeping tiger.

"Russell what did you do? What did you do!" Amy was panicking, talking at a frenetic pace. "Is he bleeding? Should we turn him over? Go get some ice! Where is there ice!?" She started breathing rapidly, then she shouted, "RUSSELL! ANSWER ME!"

But he didn't. He couldn't. Russell was looking at the polar bear.

His brain refused to process the image he saw through the glass.

Amy had just decided she would slap him to see if *that* would wake him up, when she saw it too. The bright red rage and panic drained from her face and her features melted into an expression of abject horror.

Amy screamed.

Her scream made his ears ring as tears streamed down her face. She screamed for so long that he didn't think she could possibly have any oxygen left, and in fact she didn't. Amy fell to her knees and hugged herself, rocking gently back and forth.

Russ approached the glass slowly, like walking in a pool. He reached out to touch the glass timidly, as if it might burn his fingers.

Unable to cope with the reality of the tableau before him, Russ's mind wandered to less relevant subjects.

Like how long it would take the zoo to get a new polar bear.

-8-

WHAT HAPPENED TO THE BEAR.

Russ could remember seeing a show once, Mr. Rogers maybe, where they were teaching kids how acrobats trained. They wore harnesses connected to a half dozen elastic cords. These cords would move with them while they swung and flipped, stopping them from hitting the floor if they fell.

That's what it made him think of. The polar bear, suspended in the air by those ropes, like a giant, white, bleeding acrobat in mid-fall. The ropes were wrapped around his legs, neck and torso, the other ends wrapped around the metal tubing of the spotlight rigging. The rigging made sort of a frame, festooned with different color lights to dazzle spectators at night.

The ropes weren't nylon or elastic, though. In fact, Russ couldn't say exactly *what* they were. They were whitish, translucent, and textured in places with a series of repeating rings, like the hose attached to a vacuum cleaner.

The head hung limply to the side, the tremendous blue tongue hanging out like that of a panting dog, and the eyes were dark and bleeding. No, not dark, he realized, *missing*. The empty sockets were leaking bright red blood down the great gray muzzle.

There was a hunk of its right shoulder missing. It was a semicircular chunk, like a bite out of a chocolate chip cookie. Instead of gooey chocolate, however, the inside of this bite was torn pink muscle, splinters of bone, a flap of furry skin, dangling strings of sinew, and creamy yellow gobs of fat. Splashing down from the wound like a sash was a crimson stain almost a foot wide. Around the edges of the wound, where the pink insides met the coarse white hair, were small, black burn marks with tiny, twisted, burnt hair.

As he looked at it, it ceased to resemble an acrobat in training and began to look more like the bear had been caught in the web of an enormous spider.

"Intestines." Amy had crept up on him again.

He looked at her, still not able to speak.

"Look. Those aren't ropes. They're intestines." she said as she pointed. The cords holding the bear up were glistening, ridged in places, almost accordion-like, and ranging in color from white to dull gray. They were also beaded with drops of blood, here and there.

He noticed something else about them; the dangling ends of the intestines were charred.

"So..." she attempted, then cleared her throat and rubbed her eyes. "So, someone hung him up with his own intestines?"

"No," Russ said, "not unless polar bears keep their intestines in their shoulder."

She saw what he meant. Though the big bear's gut was spattered and streaked with blood, it was still closed.

"You mean they hung him up with intestines from another animal?" she asked.

"Well," he said, gazing up at the bear, "let's *hope* it was an animal."

-9-

I'M GETTING OUT OF HERE

"Who... how..." Russ stammered before asking the most perplexing question: "Why?"

"I have no idea, but I'm getting out of here!" she snapped.

"What?" he exclaimed. "Don't you want to find out, I mean, don't you want to see..." As Russ talked in the shadow of the grisly bear, he was becoming less convinced that he wanted to see or find out anything about what had caused it. Still, the zoo represented a mystery, an adventure, while leaving meant the certainty of school, detention, and grounding.

"No way!" she said, folding her arms. She began to sound like a scolding parent or teacher. "Russell Yamhill, you can fart around all you want with blood and guts and cops and all that, but I'm going home!"

"But.." he interjected, as was immediately cut off.

"For-GET it, kid!" she said, increasing in volume. "*You* can hang out and find out what or who can lift a full-grown polar bear in the air, tie it up with another animal's intestines, take a huge *bite* out of it, and, and..." she was becoming too angry to speak.

"But there's cops everywhere! It's safe! What's going to happen with all those cops around?" he pleaded.

"Oh, GREAT!" she shouted. "Hear that, Teddy?" she screeched, addressing the bear. "Look at all these cops! You're SAFE! No need to WORRY! And..." she paused, taking a breath as she experienced fresh shock.

"Look," he said, holding his hands up, palms out.

"What happened to his EYES!?" she screamed.

Before he could reply, she spun and power-walked toward the exit. Russ felt he needed to sit, close his eyes, and think, maybe for an hour. He just couldn't make any sense of anything. Maybe it would be better to just give up and go home and be safe.

Russell David Yamhill just wasn't ready to give up yet.

However, given her decisiveness, he really had no choice at that moment but to scamper after her. He could see by the forward slant of her features that it was useless talking to her, so he just trotted along beside her.

As they rounded the corner of a sno cone stand, they caught sight of the maintenance man, the baggy guy with the moustache and pushcart full of cleaning supplies. He was crouching low beside the hyenas, inside the "DO NOT CROSS" railing for spectators, just outside the fence. He seemed to be listening intently.

Amy walked right up to him, ducking under the railing to stand beside him. "Excuse me," she said, "we're lost."

The man didn't move.

"Lost *children*?" she insisted, hands on her hips.

His head turned to look at her so swiftly she was startled. He shot a momentary look at Russ, then refocused on Amy with eyes like glaciers, pale and whitish-blue. His stare was unbelievably serious, as if he was demanding that she justify her very existence on the planet, much less her egregious interruption. The bushy mustache was gone, revealing the most severe face Russ had ever seen.

"I.. uh..." Amy was powerless. Russ just watched.

Without taking his eyes from her, and without making a sound, the man reached a hand into his cart and grabbed a small black case. His arm moved with silent fluidity, like an octopus tentacle.

He undid a buckle and opened the case, revealing a set of immaculate black metal tubes, like gun barrels, resting in foam notches.

The man's gaze was still aimed at Amy, his cold, unblinking eyes transfixing her. The gravity of his expression made her feel more like a scolded child than she ever had in her entire life.

His fingers worked quickly, deftly screwing two of the tubes together. When he was finished, he held the combined tube up to his left eye and turned back to scan the hyena den.

Without those eyes bearing down on her, Amy regained a little of her composure. "Um, sir? We're..."

She was interrupted by his thumb, which he jerked over his shoulder with alarming speed, pointing it in the direction of the exit. The way his arm moved, Russ was sure he could have killed a man with that thumb.

"But..." she began.

"Shut up. Leave." His voice was like sandpaper on gravel.

She shuffled meekly off, thoroughly admonished, though she couldn't say exactly what for. Russ caught up to her.

Russ saw two cops about a hundred yards down the path. He was ready for her to hail them so they could leave safely, to face his angry teacher and disappointed parents.

Suddenly, she stopped and turned to face him.

"Nobody tells me to shut up!" she said.

He rolled his eyes. He wanted to tell her to shut up too, but decided against it. "Well, what are you gonna do? I mean, who was that guy? Not zoo maintenance, I'm pretty sure."

But she wasn't listening. She had the faraway stare of someone searching her own thoughts. "Come on," she said, "let's go."

"Where?" he asked, sick of her dragging him around.

"To the back of the hyena cage."

It was a cool idea. She wanted to see up-close what Shut-Up Man was peering at through his little telescope thing. Just as he was thinking this, he noticed the two cops had seen them and were walking toward them.

-10-

TRAPPED

"Amy! They saw us!" Russell looked frantically over his shoulder and back at Amy. "Come on!"

Amy's head snapped around to see the two cops walking toward them, their pace increasing.

Russ lead the way. The hyena cage was a triangle, with its apex wedged in the intersection of a Y-shaped path. Russ jogged along the side opposite the one where they'd bumped into Blue Eyes.

They reached the corner and crawled into the thick weeds, almost woods, behind the third side of the cage. Russ saw the Hyenas, fast asleep of course, against the chain link. He hoped they'd evaded the cops, though something told him there was no hope of sneaking past the blue-eyed man.

One of the hyenas must have been awake somewhere; Russ could just make out a soft clicking noise, probably the animal chewing a flea bite.

They stayed low and still, watching the cops make their way to the back of the cage, one walking along each side. The hyena cage backed up to the edge of the zoo, so there was nowhere left to run or hide.

And maybe they should stop running, anyway, Russ supposed. He was not Fred, and Amy wasn't Velma. This was not a silly TV mystery cartoon, and there was no happy ending. No matter how he tried to forget it, at the end of this day he had detention, grounding, and probably worse punishments waiting for him, and there was no getting out of it. Just like the two police rounding the back corners of the hyena cage, it was inevitable.

Russ and Amy shared a look, one that seemed to communicate these realities, one that said, *playtime is over.*

They stood up together, slowly, sensing that it might be a bad idea to surprise police. The cops were slowly converging on them through the tangle of weeds and branches.

"What are you kids doing back here?" asked the first cop to reach them. He didn't wait for an answer, which was a relief to Russ. "Let's go, we gotta get you outta here." He pulled a walkie-talkie from his belt.

Before he could begin speaking into it, though, his partner interrupted: "Ted! Ted look at these!" The other cop was crouching beside the sleeping hyenas.

Ted walked past Russ and Amy to join his partner. "Oh my…" He was silently shaking his head. Both cops were staring at the hyenas, mouths open.

Russ and Amy both noticed at the same time. They weren't sleeping. They were dead. Each one was lying on its side and displaying a long gash down its belly.

"What did you kids *do*!? What are you doing back here?!"

"WHAT!?" shouted Amy. "You think *we* did this? Are you insane!?"

Russ glanced through the trees and brush at the man on the far side of the cage. The blue eyes were fixed so still their bearer may have been a statue. But they weren't looking as Russ, or Amy or the cops. The man seemed to be studying a large stump. Russell looked to Amy, to see if she had noticed the man, but she was busy being indignant at the cop's accusation. He looked back, and the man was gone, disappeared.

Amy's rant ran out of steam; she seethed.

The two cops looked at eachother, then walked a few paces away to confer quietly. Amy sighed deeply, awaiting and end to the whole ordeal in the near future. Russ's anxiety about blood and guts subsided and was gradually replaced with anxiety about school.

He walked over to the hyena corpses, where he still heard the clicking noise. It sounded a little like when his own dog was licking herself, and, since hyenas are dogs, that's what he expected to see. But there were no live hyenas in the cage at all.

He craned his neck to see over the stump, from where, he was pretty sure, the clicking noise was emanating. At first it looked like snakes, a writhing tangle of them.

Suddenly, as if they sensed they were being watched, they all froze, looking almost like the brown branches of a dead tree, and the clicking stopped. They slowly rose.

As they revealed themselves, Russ saw that they were connected at the base, more like tentacles than snakes. They seemed to be rooted in some kind of metal plate, which came into view as more of a dome. The rim of the dome, like the lip of an upside-down salad bowl, just barely crested the top of the stump, showing only darkness beneath.

Then, a bright red light shone out from under the rim, and Russ noticed a web of red laser lights moving slowly over the backs of the cops. He wanted to warn them, but what would he say? Russ had no words for what was happening, much less what he was afraid might happen next. He didn't have to wait long to find out.

In a flash of gleaming metal and whirling brown tentacles, the thing flew out from behind the stump, burst through the chain link fence and attached itself to Ted's hip.

Ted screamed.

-11-
THEY'RE EVERYWHERE

Ted twisted in panic trying to shake it off. The thing, whatever it was, was a writhing mass of grasping tentacles, shining metal fuselage, and scrabbling cancrine legs. The metal center, almost like a flying saucer the size of two punch bowls, was split along its equator, and it was between the two hemispheres that Ted's leg was trapped.

The other cop fumbled with the snap on his holster, drew his gun and aimed it with trembling hands.

"DON'T SHOOT! LENNY! DON'T SHOOT!" Ted screamed in agony. Whatever was happening to his leg, it hurt.

The monstrosity stopped moving and aimed its laser light at Lenny's arms, then focused on his gun. In the moments it was still, Russ could see it more clearly. There was a medusa-like tangle of tentacles emerging from the top of a sleek, metal ellipsoid. Around the center, there was a dark gap in the metal. The thing was propelling itself with segmented legs like those on a crab or a tarantula, if that tarantula had been the size of a large dog. He couldn't count the legs or tentacles, but it seemed like there were at least a dozen of each.

With a noise like a band saw, it closed on Ted's hip. Ted's leg fell one way, the rest of Ted fell the other way, both wounds trailing smoke and glowing with embers.

Amy's scream ripped fresh wounds in Russ's eardrums, and Lenny started firing, two, three, four shots, POP-POP-POP-POP!

He probably meant to keep shooting, but the thing was on him, tangling both arms in its tentacles before snapping the two halves of its metal body shut on his hands. Lenny shredded the air with a hoarse scream and fell to his knees like he was praying to an alien god of octopi and arachnids.

Thin tendrils of smoke began to rise from the dark center of the beast, and then it dropped to the concrete, landing light as a cat on those horrible, bristled legs. Lenny was silently shivering, staring with disbelief at his smoldering stumps.

Russ wanted to run but couldn't. He was rooted to the spot with the fear that running would excite the creature, make it want to hunt him and separate him from one of his four favorite limbs. Amy was useless, all out of screams but just staring at nothing, pale and swaying.

It quickly skittered toward Russ and Amy, stopping ten paces short of them and waving its tentacles slowly. Intense red light flared at them as it swept its laser up and down their bodies.

Russ was trying to decide whether to run, try to kick the thing, or just give up, as Amy apparently had, when it opened and launched something at them. Russ dove, tackling Amy, out of the way of the… the what? The bomb? The net? Spear?

Hands over the back of his head, he heard the legs clicking on the concrete, receding down the path in the direction of the zoo entrance. He looked up to see what the thing had fired at them and was puzzled for a moment, unsure of what to make of the blackened, smoking, twisted shapes.

"Oh my…" Amy said softly. "Those are his *hands*." She was right. Russ could make out the shapes of fingers, the ends of sleeves, even the gun Lenny had been holding. Russ looked over to Officer Lenny, who slumped to the concrete, as unconscious as Ted. Strangely, neither seemed to be bleeding. He was thinking of checking for a pulse, feeling for breathing, something like that, when Amy grabbed him by the elbow and yanked him to his feet.

Russell just stood and stared.

"Come on," she said, "we should have gotten out of here a *long* time ago."

She marched through the brush toward the entrance with great purpose in her strides. Russell stared at the hands and thought.

Shortly after, he caught up with Amy.

"Where were you?"

"I was…"

"Whatever. *Never mind*."

His head began to clear, and he realized what a joy detention would be, what pleasure grounding, what sublime ecstasy having his video games taken away would seem compared to having that thing sever one of his limbs. Amy was right, they needed to leave, and they were doing that.

He breathed a deep sigh, yanked his elbow away from Amy, and matched her stride for confident stride in her march out of the zoo. He even smiled, imagining that this would most likely be his last ever field trip to the stupid, stank zoo.

He stopped so suddenly he needed to dig both heels into the pavement, and he threw an arm across Amy's middle, stopping her too. She wheeled around and slapped him full in the face, hard. He could see little pinpricks of light in his vision and the right side of his face began to swell immediately.

He rubbed his face with one hand and pointed with the other. Amy turned to look. Near the big brick monkey house, where the path widened and made a U around the semicircular rhinoceros enclosure, there was an alligator. It's head and forelegs were emerging from a clump of bushes beside the path. It was very still, but Russ knew that was how they hunted.

Then, it moved backward. It didn't walk, or crawl, or even slither. It just moved with a faint scraping noise on the concrete. Russ tiptoed out to see around a bush, and there it was: the squid-robot-tarantula thing, tentacles wrapped around the tail, struggling to drag the weight of the massive reptile.

Russ snuck backward, slowly. Then he heard it again: the clicking noise. Except it was different this time, because it was multiplied many times. It sounded like half a dozen of them, approaching quickly from the woods on the far side of the path.

Russ ran, past Amy, into the building housing the cockroaches. Amy followed close behind, and they peered out a circular window to see it. Another one. Another two, then three more. Seven of the things crawling nimbly across the path.

Then, a hundred more. At least. A herd of them, like a grotesque cattle drive, flowed across the walkway. They went into the monkey house. In the doors, through the bars of the external cages, Even trying to run right up the smooth concrete walls, though falling backward in the attempt.

They had appeared and then were out of sight in less than ten Mississippis.

Russ said a word that was inappropriate for third grade.

-12-
SHELTER

"Okay," said Amy, taking a deep breath, steeling herself. "The exit is right over there," and she pointed past the monkey house to the revolving bars of the one-way exit. There was an empty chair beside it, where, usually, you expected to see a zoo employee stamping people's hands for re-entry. The souvenir shop, the ice cream cart, the balloon stand, all empty.

The parking lot was empty as well. Russell had expected to see police cars, fire engines, helicopters, army vehicles: the works. Russ found their absence unsettling in the extreme.

Amy's breathing got louder, and Russ could tell she was planning to sprint for the exit. He guessed he would have to go with her, or else be trapped in the zoo with giant tarantula-legged squid-bots. With lasers. He looked down at his hands, imagining them getting sawed off by whatever was hidden inside those things.

Amy's breathing stopped, and her mouth opened. A half dozen of them scuttled out one of the side doors to the monkey house and stopped, sweeping their red laser lights in wide arcs. Within a minute, the next door down showed a similar display, and Russ would be willing to bet that all of the other doors to the monkey house had them, too.

"What are they doing?" Amy asked in a faint whisper.

"Sentries," said Russ.

"What?" she asked, looking at him as if he had just spoken in Greek.

Russ rolled his eyes. "Guards. You know, lookouts?"

The way she flicked her hair back indicated that she didn't appreciate his condescending tone. "Do you think we can sneak past them to the exit? I mean, it looks like they're just guarding the doors to the building."

Russ visualized walking past them. The zoo achieved a bottleneck around the monkey house, with only about 15 feet of leeway on either side, then tall fences. He looked back at his hands, opening and closing them.

"No," he said. "I don't think we can."

"The fence?"

Russ looked at it and thought. He wasn't really sure how tall it was, because about 12 feet off the ground it disappeared into branches of conifers on both sides of the border. He imagined getting halfway up the fence, then getting caught by one of the things. At least on land he could run away.

Amy must have had similar thoughts, because the subject was dropped.

Russell looked around the dimly-lit interior of the otter building. Besides the big window looking over and under the otter pond, there was a strange combination of animals: cockroaches, tortoises, sturgeon, and a six-foot cubic terrarium housing the albino boa constrictor, lit from above by a skylight. This building was his favorite place in the zoo. He wouldn't have told Amy, or anyone, but he was glad to be trapped in such a comforting place.

"Do you think we'll be safe in here until it's over?" she asked.

"I don't know, I guess so," he said. "Actually," he continued, "I don't see why they couldn't get in here. They seem, I don't know, smart in a way. Like dolphins or wolves, like they can hunt as a pack, cooperate."

Amy's brow twisted in revulsion. Russ tried to guess which of the things he had just said offended her.

He looked out the window facing the monkey house again. He also wondered where they could go, what they could do. Would this whole thing just be *over* at some point? Would the end come soon enough that they could wait it out here?

"Dolphins don't hunt!" she said accusingly. "They eat *fish*!"

It took him a full five seconds to even begin understanding her ignorance. "What?"

"Wolves kill rabbits and eat them, but dolphins are kind! When's the last time you saw a dolphin kill something?"

He opened his mouth to begin lecturing her on the dozen or so ways in which she was wrong, then closed it again. She was scared, stressed, and talking crazy. He had no chance of getting through to her, and correcting her would only make her madder.

Maybe it was the stress of the day, but she just had to keep prodding him on. "What Russell, WHAT!"

He couldn't take it, he'd tried to be nice, but he was stressed too. "Just because you think of bunnies as cute and because you probably don't even think of fish as prey animals and just because you think dolphins are so adorable you'll probably get a *tattoo* of one on your ankle some day doesn't mean that…"

He was interrupted by a tapping sound. Faint at first, it became louder and more resonant. Neither of them could quite tell where it was coming from as they frantically scanned the windows.

Then, the series of knocks ended with the tinkling of broken glass. They both looked at the python cage at once, seeing a segmented, bristled leg reach tenuously down through the hole in the skylight.

-13-
CONTACT

Amy clamped both hands over her mouth to stifle a scream and Russ darted behind the sturgeon tank. Amy joined him, and together they watched between the slow-moving fish.

The leg seemed to be searching, feeling blindly for a floor, then it retracted. Three more knocks on the skylight, much louder than the previous batch, and it came crashing down into the python terrarium, landing nimbly on its feet in a cascade of shattered glass.

Through murky water and the pale, tapered bodies of the sturgeon, they could see the red glare of the laser scanning methodically around the room.

Amy slowly stood, peering over the top of the tank. Russ grabbed her hand, trying to pull her back down, but she broke his grip with a jerking motion that also smacked him in the head. She walked slowly out from behind the tank and toward the python case.

It noticed almost immediately, and Amy was bathed in crisscrossed grid lines of red laser. She moved forward, slowly, but not faltering.

Russell considered making a break for it, sneaking out while the thing was focused on Amy. However, he couldn't bring himself to do it, imagining her disgust at his cowardice. He found it maddening that he would even care what she thought, as he was pretty sure he hated her guts.

She stood about a foot from the glass, staring, fists clenched. The laser turned off, and the thing stood stone-still on the opposite side.

Amy reached out and tapped on the glass three times. Just a minute prior, Russell hadn't thought she could be any stupider. But here she was. Tapping again, *tap-tap-tap*.

One of the terrible, too-big tarantula legs reached carefully for the glass, as if not sure where exactly it was, and tapped three times. Amy, gaining confidence, reached up and tapped five times. It responded almost immediately: *tap-tap-tap-tap-tap*.

She raised a hand, palm out, and waved. The foreleg that was still raised for tapping, began to move slowly back and forth, like a windshield wiper on low.

It was waving back.

Russ got low, below the glass of the aquarium, and inched out from behind it on elbows and knees, trying not to let even his breath make a sound. Amy continued her slow-motion, silent game of Simon Says with one of the creatures that had, not ten minutes ago, hewn extremities from two grown men.

Russ was no ninja; Amy spotted him. So did the creature, and he was awash in the laser light, prone on the carpet. He figured he might as well just stand up. Amy shot him a furious glance, letting him know he was messing up. He was tired of feeling stupid, though, and decided not to care. Feeling bold, he approached the python glass.

"Hey dude!" he said, waving. It did not wave back. In fact, it did not stop scanning him, either. The red light narrowed in scope, and focused brightly on his bulging left pocket.

"Russell," said Amy as if she was talking to a toddler, "just walk away, and…"
It launched itself at the glass, hitting with the curved metallic prow of its midsection. The glass cracked, and it crouched for another spring. BOOM! It hit the glass again, denting its chrome hull and falling backward. The pane was a busy roadmap of cracks, bulging slightly at the site of the impact. It was getting up, wavering in its gait as it positioned itself for another try. The last it would need, Russ figured

-14-

FROM ALL SIDES

He grabbed Amy's arm and ran out the door. The outside greeted them with lungfuls of syrupy heat as their shoes slapped hot asphalt. No path was safe, not the path back, nor the path forward on either side of the monkey house, and definitely not *through* the monkey house.

Russ let go of Amy and vaulted the wooden post fence around the rhino enclosure. The fence wouldn't have held a dog, much less a rhino. What contained them was a deep, smooth moat just inside the fence.

Russ slid into it, maybe eight feet down, and lay still. Amy's head peeked over the precipice and shout-whispered, "Russ! Russ what are you doing!"

"Come on!" he shouted, not caring about the noise. He got up and jogged around the curve until he found what he was looking for: the ladder. They were small rungs, about six inches each, set into the nearly vertical wall of the moat. Russ started climbing.

"Ow!" he heard from behind him as Amy landed awkwardly in the moat. She started climbing after him. "Okay Mr. Smartypants, what can you tell me about rhinoceroses? Lemme guess, even though they're ugly and scary, they're really just big, sweet hippos?"

Russell could have told her that hippos were extremely aggressive and would attack and kill humans, and that rhinos were completely unpredictable and might charge at anything at any time. However, he objected to the name "Mr. Smartypants," so he said nothing and kept climbing. He just hoped the rhinos were sleeping.

As he crested the inner moat wall, he saw that they were not. They were on the opposite side of the enclosure, though, and might not notice him. He tiptoed toward the ladder up the side of the monkey building, Amy close behind. Halfway there, Amy said, "Aww! They're kind of cute!"

They were spotted. Two enormous gray heads pivoted to look at them, and there was a snort that resonated like distant thunder.

"Russ!" she whispered, "what do we do? Do we stay still? Walk slow? Run?"

He was furious with her for asking a question to which he did not know the answer. He looked at the rhinos for any clue regarding their intention, but found none; his knowledge of them didn't include body language. One of them suddenly blazed with red light. Laser light.

The thing was standing on the far edge of the moat, scanning each one of them in turn: male rhino, female rhino, Amy, and then Russ.

Before he had time to even hope that it wouldn't be able to navigate the smooth sides of the moat, it leapt effortlessly across and was scrambling toward them. Russ and Amy both broke for the monkey house ladder. There was a thunderous drumbeat and Russ was too frightened to look back and see what terrible weapon the thing was preparing for them. Amy's foot landed in a pile of dung and she slipped, falling forward and grabbing Russ' ankle on her way down so they both sprawled on the rough sculpted concrete of fake rocks. Ignoring the pain of numerous scrapes and bruises as well as the rhythmic thunder, they both scrambled to their feet just in time for the thing to catch up with them and make a leap for Russ.

-15-

HIGHER GROUND

He saw the wriggling mass of tentacles and legs silhouetted against the bright June sky as it descended upon him. His mind flashed back to hours upon hours staring at patterns in the floor tiles at school while the teacher droned on and on, then to a montage of hundreds of disappointed looks on the faces of various adults in his life. At that moment, he couldn't have said if such a bleak summary made his imminent death easier or harder to face, but the certainty of it enveloped him.

The thunder increased, and he was sure it must be the sound of his blood pumping with mortal fervor at the point of his demise.

The earth shook.

And the thing was not on him rending his limbs, it was squirming spasmodically against the brick of the monkey house, pinned there by an irate rhino. Russ watched slick, black fluid leak down the pale beige beige brick as it lashed its slippery tentacles against the rhino with decreasing frequency. The shiny fuselage was a crumpled metal blossom at the end of the tremendous gray horn.

The world was mercifully silent for seven wonderful seconds.

"Russ!" screamed Amy, pointing. The other rhino was facing them and broke into a gallop. It was shocking how rapidly it got all four thousand pounds into motion. Amy jumped and grabbed the bottom rung of the ladder and began climbing.

Russ jumped and narrowly missed the bottom rung. He got it on his second try and pulled with all of his might, difficult because he was so weak and he couldn't use his legs to help until he was a few more rungs along.

The rhino was there and russ swung his legs up and out of the way as it scored a glancing blow against the building and continued in a wide arc, preparing for another charge.

Russ found the strength to pull himself up until his legs could engage the ladder too and began to scramble up the side of the building. He was more than halfway up when the rhino struck again, this time managing to detach the rusted metal bolts that held the ladder to the bricks, and Russ' world spun and lurched as the bottom of the ladder swung away from the wall.

Climbing became ten times more difficult as the ladder swayed beneath his feet and hands. Plus, with the stress, the hot weather, and the scorching metal rungs, Russ was sweating enough to make the ladder feel as if it was coated in bacon grease.

One rung from the top he slipped, knocking his chin on the penultimate rung and flailing madly to reconnect with the ladder.

-16-

LUCKY BOY

The ground didn't rush up to meet him, it just swung sickeningly to and fro thirty feet below his flailing feet. He inadvertently kicked one of his sneakers off and watched it tumble down and smack the already annoyed male rhino in the head.

He looked up and saw that his arm was in the grasp of a thick, leather-gloved hand.

"Pull!"

Whoever said it, Russ obeyed and was hauled up. Lungs heaving with exhaustion, grateful to be alive, Russ lay flat against the scorching gravel-and-tar roof. He had never given thought to just how magnificent it was to be on solid ground, but at that moment all he wanted to do was embrace it and never leave it again.

-17-
WACKO ON THE ROOF

He slowly woke up to a beautiful summer day. He was in a comfortable folding deck chair under an umbrella. The sun was shining and it was hot, but there was a pleasant breeze tickling between his bare toes. He looked down to his right; there was even a cooler, maybe stocked with sodas and popsicles. He reached up to rub his face, and he felt the gravel embedded in his cheek. It all suddenly came back to him, and he let out a long, tired breath in despair.

He was still on the roof, and Amy was still with him. She seemed to be conferring with some bear-shaped person on the shady side of a shed. He looked down at his bruised and scraped body, and the physical rigor he'd endured made itself known in a pervasive bodily ache.

When he tried to get up, he found that the other overwhelming souvenir of the day's trials was an incredible stiffness. Every move he made felt as if it was restrained by bungee cords. Russ groaned.

That got the attention of the bear-person, whose head snapped around to see him. "He's coming to!" it said with the gravity of a soldier saving the world in an action movie.

She sprinted to his side and held out a dented canteen. "Here! Drink this!" she said with the same urgency as if she was telling him to get rid of a live grenade.

Stocky legs, cargo shorts, army-surplus shirt and a pith helmet with the strap tied taut under her substantial chin, eyes blazing with urgency: it was the zoo guide.

Russ groaned again as he reached for it, the muscles in his arm complaining.

"No!" she barked at him. "Here…" She held the canteen up to his mouth and started pouring. It smelled like when old people breathed on him at church, and he knocked it away and sat up.

"You've got to get hydrated! You may be in shock!"

"There's bottled water in the cooler," Amy said, pointing.

The guide looked shocked and deeply hurt, until Amy said "But you really should drink something." Feeling somewhat validated, the guide went back to the shady spot beside the shed.

"That's Pat," said Amy. "She's quite serious about this."

Russ rolled his eyes and reached for the cooler, and Pat yelled over to him, "Those are our emergency rations! We may need those to last us a while!" Rus lifted the lid. It was packed full with bottled water, five wide, twelve long, and probably at least three deep. Russ yaked one out and started gulping; it was the best thing he had ever tasted.

"You OK?" Amy looked genuinely concerned.

"Yeah," Russ said, "I mean, I guess. What happened? Did I hit my head or something?"

"I don't think so. Just after you got up here you laid down and went to sleep. We moved you to shade…"

"Why is there the umbrella and…" Russ said and gestured to the cooler and chair. Pat was hunched down, moving rocks around as if playing chess with herself.

"I asked and she just said 'You *must* be prepared!' She's a little…" Amy tapped the side of her forehead.

"Ya think?" Russ finished the water and reached for another.

"Um," said Pat, loud enough to stop him. "That's, uh…"

Not wanting to hear more about it, Russ left the cooler closed.

"She's going to tell you about her plans," said Amy, her voice low. "Just listen and nod. And good Lord do not ask her about the bathroom."

"Why, we can't get to it?"

"No, she made one. She *showed* me." Amy shuddered faintly in disgust.

"Alright guys," Pat called to them, "we really need to get to work on a strategy here."

Russell slowly lifted his body out of the chair. Amy held his elbow to help steady him, which made him feel like an invalid. He yanked it away and she rolled her eyes. Pat was talking in low, staccato bursts into her box of animal crackers. It sounded to Russ like whatever animal lived in there wasn't being soothed so much as given orders.

When they joined Pat beside the shed, she quickly held the box to her chest with one hand and pointed at the ground with the other. "You two get oriented while I finish this up." She raised the box back up to the side of her face and resumed the conversation. Russ thought he heard the her say "Mister President" somewhere in there. Weird name for a pet.

She had laid out twigs, rocks, and detritus from the roof in an elaborate pattern. "Okay," said Amy, "this is us here." She pointed to two pebbles and a plastic bottle cap in a rectangle made of sticks. Russ recognized the layout as an amazingly accurate map of the zoo. Every inch of it, from parking lot to back gate in fine detail.

"She made all of this?"

"Yes." Amy nodded, eyes wide. "She most definitely did."

Russell crouched to examine it, and started replaying the morning's events at different locations on the map. "Well," he said, "I guess this means we're safe or something." He figured that a grownup, even one like Pat, was good news and that all would be taken care of. It was a relief.

"I'm not really sure about that actually."

Russ let that comment go. He wasn't interested in further conflict of any kind.

"So what do you think is in that box? A cricket? Maybe a vole or something?"

Amy clamped her lips tightly and vigorously shook her head.

"What? There's little air holes poked in it. I'd say cricket for any normal person, but…"

Amy's panicked eyes looked over his shoulder, then skyward. Russ looked around with considerable pain in his neck, half expecting to see one of those things approaching. It was just Pat.

"What's this now?" she asked, clutching the box in her left hand.

"What you got in the box? Cricket?"

Pat looked bewildered. Russ pointed at the box. "Cricket?"

Pat looked at the box and back at Russell as if he had snakes slithering out of his nostrils. "Son," she said, then stopped.

Russ looked at Amy, who had her hand over her face.

"Son, I don't know if I should be telling you this, in fact I'm sure I shouldn't. However in light of your recent trauma and seeing as how you seem to be delusional and or delirious, possibly experiencing P.T.S.D., I'll tell you that this here is an emergency line directly to…" Pat paused, lowered her head between her shoulders, narrowed her eyes, and scanned left and right as if expecting someone to be listening.

"…to the Commander in Chief." She straightened her neck and resumed her military posture.

"What, Barack Obama?"

Amy's eyes rolled so high it looked like she was trying to scrape her pupils on the roof of her skull. She had heard this already.

"Shh!" said Pat, and she immediately clamped a meaty palm across Russell's mouth. "That's classified!"

She released him and turned smartly on her heel to face the map. Amy threw her hands up as if to say *I tried to tell you*. Russ realized that they were definitely not out of this.

"Now it's hard to know where they'll be," Pat said.

"They?" said Russ.

Pat looked at him and narrowed her eyes. "The hostiles," she said, pronouncing it to rhyme with "miles." "Here is the nearest evac point, and these lines here represent the shortest lines of retreat." Pat was busily indicating different parts of her map with a stubby finger. The escape routes, along either side of the monkey house, were made from red twist ties.

Russ looked at Amy quizzically. "*Evacuation* point," Amy explained.

"Now," Pat said, adjusting her belt, "there are possible safe zones here, here, and here." Russ recognized the various structures as she pointed to them.

"That one's not safe," Russ said. "One of those things broke in through the skylight."

Pat squinted at him in confusion.

"One of the *hostiles*," Russ said, and Pat nodded curtly. She reached in one of the bulging pouches in her cargo shorts and pulled out a straw wrapper. She fiddled with it as she talked.

"The other two locations offer the possibility of replenished rations, but the roof here gives us the best possible tactical advantage."

While she had been talking, Pat had make a neat white X out of the straw wrapper and secured it with a stone on the rectangle representing the otter building. She picked up a series of yellow twist ties which, Russ realized, represented lines of retreat.

Amy and Russ shared a brief, panicked look. This was a crazy person.

-18-

BLAME

Pat explained her thoughts and plans with a fervor that told Russ she had probably been waiting her whole life for something like this to happen. She seemed to enjoy emergency the way some people enjoyed hot fudge sundaes.

She was eager to mount a daring and complex retreat to the animal hospital. One of the major advantages of that *facility* was the *meds* available there in case of possible *casualties*. Amy and Russ nodded politely as Pat went into great and gory detail about *field dressing*.

When Russ asked how they would get down without the ladder, Pat explained how the shed was actually the top of a staircase that went down the middle of the building with an exit into one of the vestibules, the one with the piranha.

Russ felt himself slipping into the role of child/student, accepting that what this person said was just the way it would be. Pat was in charge. He hated himself for being such a coward, but he was unable to do anything but follow orders.

When Pat was finally finished, she began dividing up the water bottles for each of them to carry and busied herself folding the umbrella and strapping it to her back. She stopped her work to receive another phone call on the animal crackers box. "Yes Mister President," she said as she turned her back to them. A few more quick words and she was back with them. "I've received word. It's the animal hospital. Let's move out!"

Amy looked at Russ as he stuffed water bottles into a sack and said, "This is nuts." He stopped and looked at her.

"Maybe, but what can we do?"

"Those things are everywhere, and they want to eat your leg off or something. At least up here we're safe."

"What do you mean *my* leg?"

"Well," said Amy, folding her arms. "They seem to like me just fine. I mean I was practically having a conversation with that one. Until it saw you."

"Well what the heck!" Russ felt the familiar sting of blame. Also familiar was the maddening sense that he had no idea what he could possibly have done wrong. It was a lifelong condition.

"I don't know, but it seems like you're always in trouble for *something*. Seems like you don't even try to do what you're supposed to most of the time."

Russ was dumbfounded by her sharply accusing tone, as well as by the accuracy of her claims. Everything was wrong with him, he knew that. But now, it seemed *everyone* knew it. Russ heaved a water bottle as hard as he could, watching it arc through the sunlight on its way to a satisfying crunch and splat 30 feet below.

"Oh awesome, that'll fix it." Amy gave him two thumbs up.

Pat was panicked. "What was that? What just happened? Are they coming? Come on move move move move move!"

"You know what," said Amy, maintaining her superior tone, "I'm not going. I'm staying here. There has to be more police or a helicopter or something eventually, and I think this is the safest spot to wait. I think going down there is nuts." She whipped around to face Russ dead on. "You do what you want. Good luck."

Pat's mind was clearly blown. She stood and stared, mouth agape, for what seemed like five minutes. Russ was frozen. It was like watching his parents fight, two people that scared him at cross purposes.

Finally, Pat got another call. Apparently the president wanted her to keep moving without them. She marched over to the shed, every pocket and pouch full to bursting, umbrella on her back, and opened the door. The umbrella made it tough for her to get through the door, but she made it with careful crouching and was gone without looking back.

Russ looked at his shoes.

-19-

DON'T LOOK DOWN

Russ was stuck.

He was glad to have Pat gone, but Amy was still there. He wanted nothing to do with her.

The roof, at least, was appealing. It was a wasteland, an empty, isolated wilderness. Except for Amy, he was alone. Which meant he was alone.

She had gone back to being an F.O.D. to him: alien, capricious and cruel.

He walked around the roof, giving her wide leeway as she leaned on the shed sipping water, not wanting to catch her eye. The skylight looked like a greenhouse, a squat glass house with a peaked roof. He went over to take a look.

The glass had a pattern etched into it, like the window on the downstairs bathroom of his house . Light could get in, but you couldn't really see what was on the other side. He put his ear up to it, and he heard a sound that was like a combination of buzzing bees and popcorn being made. He couldn't be sure if maybe it was just the air conditioning system.

The glass that sloped up to make the roof of the greenhouse was smooth, he noticed. He would have to climb up and over the vertical portion, which was about five feet tall. Climbing glass was an iffy proposal, but he convinced himself that, in order to withstand the elements, possibly even heavy loads of snow, this glass must be especially durable and able to hold his 65 or so pounds.

He looked back at Amy, as if he were about to try to get away with something he oughtn't, but she was resigned and oblivious.

The metal frame holding the panes gave his fingertips just enough purchase to pull up, inch by inch. His shoulders were reminding him about the business on the ladder.

Feeling his arms about to give out, Russ swung a leg out and caught his heel on the frame. He was able to push himself up, lying facedown on the smooth glass. It was an unsettling view, 30 or 40 feet up from the floor in the center aisle of the monkey house with no visible barrier to his descent and death.

However, it wasn't just the floor, or the height, that caused his blood to run cold. Russ was too terrified by what he saw to even breathe.

Amy seemed to have noticed him, splayed out atop the skylight. She shook her head in disgust. "What are you doing!" It wasn't a question, just an observation: you're an idiot.

Russ didn't dare reply. His eyes bugged wide at what was happening below. He wanted to flee but was afraid that any movement would attract their attention.

Frustrated not only by the stupidity of his precarious climb but also by the lack of response, Amy got up and trudged over to the skylight. She was beside him, hand on hips. "Well!?"

Very slowly, very carefully, Russ lifted one hand from its place on the glass. He carefully formed it into a pointing finger and gestured, ever so slightly, downward.

She cupped her hands around her temples and leaned against the etched glass. "I can't see anything!" She sighed loudly. "Just tell me, dummy!"

After a period of silence, she said, "Fine," and started climbing the glass beside Russ. When she got up there, she inhaled deeply, and Russ was terrified she might scream. Instead, she faintly squeaked a word that Russ has once gotten detention for uttering in the cafeteria.

-20-
WELCOME TO THE MONKEY HOUSE

It almost looked like river flowing, or an aerial view of complex highway system. There were hundreds, maybe thousand of the things, flowing in synchronous columns and curves, over, under, and around each other. Barely an inch of the yellow tiled floor could be glimpsed beneath the hideous, trundling horde of limb-severing monstrosities. Red laser light bled from between gleaming chrome hulls, scrabbling legs, and waving tentacles, sweeping over every surface of the interior.

Except the roof. They didn't seem interested in the roof. At least not yet.

If they had, they would have scanned two very wide-eyed figures pressed up against the glass of the skylight, lying utterly motionless. Russ imagined that, from the underside, they must have looked like a shrink-wrapped package of meat at the supermarket. And that's how he felt: a fresh, juicy morsel for the hungry hive below.

Amy reached carefully over and gently tapped the back of his hand. Russ didn't make any move or noise to respond, he didn't dare. Who knew how well those things could hear?

The tapping became more insistent, though, and he could tell she wasn't about to let up. Slowly, he turned his head to face her. She was gesticulating with her lips and her right hand. He failed to catch her meaning.

This frustrated her, and she began to repeat the same twirling gesture with her hand with increased vigor, and mouthed the words she was trying to convey more slowly and severely, eyes filling with rage.

His continued failure to understand caused her so much frustration that she momentarily forgot her fear at the scene below and yelled, "Let's slide down slowly, *Russell*!"

Just as she finished shrieking his name, the skylight blazed with red laser light, a blinding column of brilliance forcing them to turn their heads and clamp their eyes shut. The glass beneath them became instantly warm.

Russ wanted to shoot her a thumbs-up, but neither could open their eyes. Russ scrambled to get off the skylight, which was difficult given his closed eyes and profuse perspiration. He guessed Amy must have done the same, and when he opened one eye a crack he saw her lighting on the roof.

He was headed after her but suddenly froze. He heard the unmistakable brittle click of cracking glass.

-21-
GERONIMO!

Russ tried to push himself down the glass, slowly and carefully applying pressure with the heels of his hands. Just as the toe of his left foot met the metal edge of the frame, he became weightless.

His mind detached from his body.

Time stopped.

He saw himself there, suspended amid a cloud of glass shards in a pillar of crimson apocalypse. Below, the creatures congregated in a growing heap, the flailing of their tentacles suspended with the rest of time.

Time to think, to consider. What was he doing here? He was at the zoo, dragged along on another field trip to a place he could barely stand with people he found intolerable. Well, mostly. There was Amy. She was a friend, sort of. Of what sort? She still seemed to hate him, yet she had known his middle name. He was immensely touched by this fact, despite himself. If he cast his mind into the future beyond this day, if there were to be any more days for him at all, he couldn't believe things would be different. He was a weirdo, and Amy had no patience for him.

She had treated him not unlike Platt did, or his parents, or most grownups he knew. *Maybe*, Russell thought, *everyone treats me like a clueless child because that's exactly what I am.* It was painful to consider, and his mind switched gears to Platt.

After she was dragged away in cuffs, an image for which he would be eternally grateful, what would happen to her? He couldn't imagine a school day without her imposing her will on the classroom. Even when there was a substitute teacher, her menace seemed to loom. He tried to take pleasure in thinking she might no longer be his teacher, but that pleasure was fleeting. What difference would a new teacher make, especially if all Platt had ever really done was tell him the truth about himself?

She wouldn't go to jail, would she? He wished she would, but then rescinded that wish when he visualized her sitting in an orange jumpsuit on a cot in a small, dank concrete cell. Why would he be compassionate toward her? Maybe she wasn't so mean, maybe he was just a chore to deal with day in and day out.

Amy. She wasn't his enemy because she wore annoying clothes, or because he knew the difference between a sea otter and a river otter and she didn't. She wasn't his friend because up was up, down was down, and they just were not friends.

Russell scanned the chamber. Cage bars bathed in the red glow cast zebra-stripe shadows on huddling, terrified primates.

And there, sitting cross-legged on a ledge between two gorilla statues, like a gargoyle, was the shadowed figure of a man. Beneath the brim of his cap, Russell could make out the only two things in the room not washed red: the left eye, and the right eye. Both of them as pale blue as ice on the arctic sea.

Russell's brain stopped letting him be awake.

-22-

REVELATIONS

Russell woke on a dingy couch in a windowless room lit by a single, dangling bulb. The room was crowded with shelves and pegboard, all stuffed with tools, bottles, and buckets. The wall opposite the couch was mostly occupied by a cluttered workbench. There was a man seated at the bench on a tall, swiveling stool. Russ was pretty sure he knew which man it was.

"Hold still." The rough voice carried so much menace in its whisper, Russ shuddered to imagine its shout. The man seemed to be working on something, Russ could hear the faint click of small machinery.

Attempting to sit up revealed an insurmountable challenge. Just leaning forward caused the world around him to teeter and blur, and his head seemed to weigh a hundred pounds. He laid back again. There was no pain or soreness, he noticed. In fact, he felt no sensation of his extremities at all.

"Can you talk yet." The man's elbows bobbed on either side of him while his hands worked out of sight.

"Uuuhh…" The grunt was all that came out, which terrified Russ. *Can't I talk? Why not?* He gave it another shot.

"I… I w-was.." It was like trying to speak with a wet sock in his mouth. "Fffff…"

"Falling. The 101's executed a perfect catch. Still, you'll have bruises."

"Hhh… Who…" That was all he could manage.

"I work for the United States Government," the man said. "I'm overseeing this project."

"Www… What…" Russell wasn't sure he could have articulated his bewilderment even if his mouth and tongue were fully functional.

"We had to do a field test," he said, still intent on whatever was on the bench before him. "See if they worked, what they could do. What they couldn't."

Russell's mind reeled at the thought that everything that had happened that day was intentional, planned ahead of time by the government.

"Www…" His mouth felt like foam rubber. He took a deep breath and tried to concentrate on each syllable. "What… about… the… b-b-b…" Russ inhaled deeply through his nostrils, then, "BEAR!"

The shout didn't seem to startle the man, but his hands ceased their movement. He turned slowly in his chair to face Russell. His face was drawn in all straight lines. There wasn't an abundance of wrinkles, but those that were there, beside his mouth, at the corners of his eyes, were deep, as if cut by shrapnel. The skin was like the leather of a jacket that had been worn in many storms.

And, of course, the eyes. It wasn't just their color or clarity; it was their stillness. They didn't seem to move at all, not even to blink.

"The REX101 is an experimental field unit, a combination of technological and biological components, built to assist ground forces in combat. Today, we're conducting a field test of its capabilities. The polar bear made an excellent adversary, good practice for the 101. As you saw, they passed the test with flying colors."

Russell's mind raced. Practice? Slaughtering a polar bear was some kind of *practice*? "B-b-but…" He breathed deeply and closed his eyes. "The intestines…"

"Hm, yes." Was that regret? Russ wasn't sure. "One of the possible uses of the 101 is as a medic, patching up soldiers on the field of battle. The medical programming led to the glitch you're talking about. One of today's takeaways, the 101 makes better infantry than it does a doctor." The man turned back to his work on the bench, sparing Russell the merciless gaze of those eyes.

"A glitch!" Russell was thrilled that his incredulity was expressed in clear English. He also noticed the feeling returning to his fingers in the form of a tingling sensation. "It was…" his mouth began to fail him once more. What he had wanted to say was that the polar bear had been such a huge, amazing creature. Polar bears were clever, powerful, resourceful animals, and killing one to test war-bots seemed as much of a waste as using gold-plated toilet paper.

"Unfortunate yes. But you've never seen war." The sureness with which it was uttered made the statement the final word in the argument. Everything Russell hated about what was going on was suddenly trivialized, the pouting of a child compared to the unknowable catastrophe of war.

"Amy…"

"She's fine. Home with her parents by now, as long as she cooperates." Russell shuddered to think what that *cooperation* entailed. Then, a statement that sent icy daggers of fear through him: "The two of you managed to see far too much today."

He realized he was a prisoner. He couldn't imagine what was in store for him, but, knowing how little regard the blue-eyed man had shown for the polar bear, he figured his chances weren't good. What if a boy who had *seen too much* was just another *glitch*? He attempted to open and close the fingers on his left hand. His arm was far too much weight to lift at first, and he struggled to get his hand into view to assess progress with muscle control.

"I think your girlfriend's reacclimation should go fine. What you need now is some rest. Don't move."

With all of his might, Russell was able to hold his hand, which felt heavier than a bowling ball, in front of his face. Open, close. Open, close.

As the man continued his work, he spoke. "We couldn't decide if it should be infantry, recon, medic, or just retrieval. 101 should be able, at least, to recover casualties." Russell imagined a soldier, wounded on a smoky field, bullets whizzing over him. Then, a tarantula-legged robot crawling to him, wrapping its tentacles around his arm, and dragging him to safety.

Suddenly, the memory of the two maimed police rose with fresh horror in his mind. "Lenny… Ted… "

"Officers Carlo and Murphy will be fine. They've been reassigned to Department business. That's about twelve promotions in one afternoon."

Russell couldn't make sense of any of this, but he hoped that the two men really were OK. Thinking about them reminded him of something, and he crafted an escape plan. He didn't know if his body or his mind would be strong enough to carry it out, but the thought of the polar bear compelled him to try.

"Th-thirsty." It was true, but also a ruse. He was sure the cold, severe man would see through it. Russell moved his left hand slowly toward his hip.

The man got up from his work and walked to a small sink in the corner to fill a paper cup. The way he moved, utterly without sound, and effortlessly, as if his limbs weighed ounces rather than pounds.

While the water ran, Russ reached down for his pocket. After the thing had chewed off Lenny's hands and spit them out at Russ and Amy, Russ had been unable to resist. He had never even seen a real gun before, not in person, much less touched one. Held one. Owned one.

He had been unable to resist prying Officer Lenny's from those blackened fingers and stuffing it in his pocket.

Now, faced with imprisonment and, for all he knew, his imminent death, he might actually have to fire one.

The blue-eyed man turned off the faucet and approached. Russ reached blindly for the gun. He desperately hoped that it was still there, and at the same time hoped it wasn't. He wasn't sure he could actually bring himself to kill a man.

The man offered Russ the paper cup. The fingers on Russell's left hand finally found metal.

-23-
BANG-BANG!

A sudden rush of adrenaline coursed through his veins, and Russ grabbed the pistol's handle, only to find it wouldn't budge. His first thought was that he was still to weak to lift it, then on further inspection he realized he wasn't touching the gun at all but something bigger, maybe even an exposed arm of the couch on which he lay prone.

His panicked eyes looked up at the man, who was holding a paper cup of tap water in one hand, and Lenny's gun in the other, pointed at Russell.

Russell was momentarily relieved that he wouldn't have to shoot anyone.

"This was your problem." The man waved the gun just slightly.

The way the man said "your problem" was, to Russell, ludicrous. As if there was only one problem, and it belonged solely to Russ. Of the myriad problems he could currently list, including school, home, the field trip, Ms. Platt, bodily injuries, and the drugged stupor he was trying to fight his way through, he couldn't imagine any single one of them that might have been caused by his gun.

His gun. It had been his, just for a short while. Heavy in his pocket, it had made him feel a little more safe, more confident, and certainly more powerful.

And now he felt the opposite of all those things.

"Might as well drink this."

Russell David Yamhill took the cup with a still-tingling hand and brought it to his lips.

His last thought was, *my leg itches*.

click

BANG-BANG!

-24-

REENTRY

Riding between soldiers in the back of the cavernous, canvas-covered truck, Amy's body finally let her feel how tired she really was. It hadn't been just the physical exertions of the day, but also the intensity of the stress. Her mind had been jerked so rapidly between extremes, she felt she had run four marathons. Maybe five. She didn't want to talk to anyone.

But the guy just wouldn't shut up.

Amy didn't want to say out loud anything that she was thinking. Experience had taught her that the less you said to grownups, the sooner they left you alone. Especially if what you had to say conflicted with what they were telling you.

"So, while hiding from your teachers…"

Russell was hiding from his teacher. I was with my mom.

"You and the boy stumbled upon our training exercise…"

We stumbled upon a polar bear with his eyes gouged out, bound to the rigging with hyena intestines.

"We were preparing in case of an event that requires emergency evacuation. Anything out of the ordinary you saw…"

You mean like a monster that can chew off a grown man's leg?

"…was part of the exercise, and not a real emergency, no matter how real or frightening it may have seemed."

Amy's mind flashed to the otter paw. The tiny, articulated fingers, the smell of burned hair. Nothing fake about that.

Also nothing fake about the crab/squid/laser things. But the guy in the suit and sunglasses was on his fourth time going through his fake explanation. Amy was trying to figure out how to shut him up, as the silent treatment wasn't working.

"Okay okay. Training exercise. Emergency evacuation. I didn't even see anything that weird or anything, just cops and soldiers and stuff."

The soldiers had come to get her off the roof about five minutes after poor Russell had fallen through the glass. She'd been a sobbing mess huddled by the shed at the top of the stairs. She tried not to think about it, because if she started crying she'd have to listen to the whole baloney story all over again.

"Look, I'm sorry I was crying. I was stressed out and wanted my mom. But I'm okay now, so, just like, okay. Everything okay."

"Oh dear," the guy said, possibly with sympathetic eyes but who knew with those dark glasses. "It's fine you were crying! Fine! No one's mad at you, sweetheart." He was about to continue but, to Amy's delight, he thought better of it and closed his mouth.

The truck got to the mall parking lot shortly after that, where Amy's parents and dozens of other people were waiting. Amy leapt off the tailgate before anyone had a chance to assist her and sprinted to her mom.

As she disappeared into a hug from both parents, she decided that the tarantula-robot things *were* imaginary, that it *was* just a training exercise. Everything she had seen that day was just too heavy a burden for her mind to bear, and, blissfully, she let it go.

Cloistered in the arms of Mom and Dad, it was easy for her to believe that everything was alright, that it would continue to be alright. As long as she didn't think about Russ.

-25-

First, there was no pain.

Russell lay still. He felt warm blood trickle down his shirt. Was that where he had been shot? In the chest? It was on his neck too. Had it splattered there, or had he caught a bullet in the neck?

His left leg itched intensely.

The only sound was ringing in his ears. It gradually became quieter, and he supposed he was dying.

The world went silent.

-26-

MA'AM PLEASE

"Ma'am, please. Ma'am. Ma'am? Ma'am. Please Ma'am."

"No, listen to me! His name is Russell David Yamhill! And he was supposed! To be on the bus! With the class! *He ran away!*"

"Ma'am, calm down. We need to ask you a few questions. Ma'am…"

"I keep telling you! He's probably still there somewhere! *Running around!*"

"Ma'am, you're charged with resisting arrest, this is serious."

"I'm charged! *I'm charged*!?"

"Ma'am? Ma'am please. When the zoo was being evacuated…"

"Was that *boy* evacuated? Russell! David! Y…"

"Yamhill, yes, we know. Ma'am please. When you struck the officer…"

"I was *trying*! To do my *job*! As a *teacher*! What is it that is so hard to understand about that!"

"Ma'am please. We're prepared to drop the charges. If you'll just cooperate. We have a few questions and then…"

"That little punk! Just gets away with *murder*! Get your hand off me! He just does whatever... *let go of me!*"

"Ma'am, we're going to have to put you back in custody until you can cooperate. Bruce? Bruce. Take her back to the pen."

"BUT HE'S STILL THERE PROBABLY! RUSSELL! DAVID! Y..."

slam!

"So, we're really not going to press charges? She hit Buckman in the jaw."

"Ha-ha! Yeah, she got him good though!"

"Geez, she's big too, looks like she coulda played linebacker. But still. She walks free? No charges?"

"No, I guess not. I got word from up above."

"From who?"

"I don't know. Somebody with pull. The order came down, someone up high told the chief, the crazy lady goes free."

"Why?"

"I don't wanna know. I don't even wanna know."

-27-

Sound returned to the world in the form of a whirring and a rhythmic click. He was still seated, but the surroundings were changing.

As focus returned, he saw the walls of a narrow concrete hallway passing rapidly on either side of him.

Wheelchair. The word flashed in his befuddled mind like subtitles. He was in a wheelchair. *Pushed by…?*

Russell craned his neck as far as he was able. He could see the strong hand on the grip, the cuff of the familiar khaki shirt. Still at the mercy of the blue-eyed man.

Still alive.

"Blanks."

The wheelchair trundled on. Russell was too tired to ask. For better or for worse, he didn't have to.

"We replaced all ammunition with blanks before the exercise began. You were never going to shoot anyone."

Russ looked down at his shirt quickly. Water. Warm water. From the cup he'd spilled right before he passed out because he had been startled. By blanks.

"Course the 101's didn't know that. They're programmed to disarm potential hostiles. They can't distinguish between live and bogus ordinance."

I bet Lenny and Ted didn't know they were blanks, Russ thought.

Relieved to at least be in control of his muscles again, he reached down to scratch his leg.

His fingernails touched metal. Right where his left leg had been, to the best of his recollection, from the moment of his birth right up until earlier that day.

"Where are we going?"

"There's a facility."

"What about..." he wasn't sure what he wanted to know. His parents? His school? His house?

The Wheelchair stopped. "Do you want to go back." It didn't sound like a question, though he supposed he was being offered a choice.

"Is it a prison?"

There was a long pause, the kind grownups take when they're trying to figure out how to break bad news to you.

"It's really up to you."

Russell's body hurt; his mind ached. His leg itched and he was starving.

"Let's just go."

The wheelchair moved forward.

-Epilog-

RUSSELL WHO?

"I heard he died!"

"From who?"

"How'd he die?"

"Is Amy like his girlfriend?"

"Wait which Amy?"

"The one from our class."

"Wait, who died?"

"Who's Russell?"

"They got left behind together or something."

"Russell who?"

"I heard they *kissed*."

"Like really? Like, *dead* dead?"

"*Noboby's dead.*" It was a ridiculous pronouncement, but Augustine Platt could make the most ludicrous words sound deadly serious, ending all discussion.

She inhaled deeply, and shifted gears into her soft, low voice, like the purring of a lioness. "Now. I'm going to my desk write an e-mail. It will take me one minute. Sixty seconds. If you're not hard at work on the social studies by the time I'm done..." There was no need for her to finish the threat verbally.

The news about Russell had the kids as squirrelly as they'd ever been. Their need to gossip about it was an elemental force.

However, the will of Platt was a massive and fearful thing, and they dared not even whisper while she typed away at her desk.

They had all seen her tackled and shackled, at the zoo. It had been easy to cheer then, a great liberation for all. However, instead of humbling her, it had only made her more loathsome. No one spoke of the incident, but they could feel her waiting for someone to try, like a child with a hammer poised over sidewalk ants.

Five minutes later, Platt was still writing. No one had finished a single question on the social studies, but no one had made a peep. Platt seemed in possession of a particularly large and angry hammer today, and she was eagerly seeking wayward ants.

She rose slowly and walked calmly front and center, hands behind her back. Her eyes scrutinized the room.

"Russell moved." All eyes were wide and fixed. She was actually talking about it. "Utah. If you would like to write to him I can get you an address."

She scanned the room, as if anyone would have actually wanted the address. Satisfied that no one liked Russ any more than she did, she continued.

"Nobody is anybody's girlfriend." Having stated this, Platt watched eagerly to see which students would turn and look at Amy. None dared.

Amy sank in her seat and wished devoutly for the school to be hit by a meteor.

Amy's family was all set to move as well; her dad had gotten transferred to England. Only three more days. England was so far, but not far enough for Amy. She would have preferred Timbuktu. Or Neptune.

As her mind replayed the movie of the boy's thin body disappearing through the broken glass for the thousandth time, she could feel her cheeks heating. What would be worse: crying or fleeing?

Emboldened by her pending move, which would place her beyond Platt's reach for good, she fled out the door and down the hall. The class stopped breathing and blinking in anticipation of Platt's rage, but Amy was allowed to leave without comment.

"ALEX!" The hammer fell, and the freckled boy jolted in his seat. "WHY do you not have even ONE question complete!" If it was possible to start a fire by rubbing pencil on paper, classroom 27 would have spontaneously ignited from the sudden fervor with which the students attacked their social studies worksheets.

FIND OUT
WHAT HAPPENED
TO RUSS IN:

BLOOD
AND
GUTS 2:

FESTERING
ZOMBIE
SPLEENS

SUMMER 2016

CONTACT

trisham.contact@gmail.com

WEBSITE

bloodandgutsbooks.com

SOCIAL MEDIA LINKS

http://facebook.com/TR.Isham.Books

Twitter: @TR_Isham

Instagram: @tr_isham

Made in the USA
Lexington, KY
25 November 2015